This Topsy and Tim book belongs to

_____

This title was previously published as part of the *Topsy and Tim Learnabout* series
Published by Ladybird Books Ltd
80 Strand London WC2R ORL
A Penguin Company

12

© Jean and Gareth Adamson MCMXCV
This edition MMIII

ISBN-13: 978-1-90435-131-3

Printed in China

Topsy+Tim
Meet the
Firefighters

Jean and **Gareth Adamson**

One morning when Topsy and Tim
were on their way to school, they
heard a fire engine coming.

It raced past them, sirens sounding and blue lights flashing. All the other traffic got out of the way. Everyone knew that the firefighters were hurrying to put out a fire.

"Kerry's dad is a firefighter," said Topsy.
"I expect he is on that fire engine."

But Kerry's dad was not on the fire
engine. It was his morning off and
he was taking Kerry to school.
Topsy and Tim told him about the
fire engine they had seen.
"They're called fire appliances, not
fire engines," said Kerry.

"There's an open day at my fire station on Saturday," said Kerry's dad. "Would you like to come and see all our fire appliances?"

"Yes, please," said Topsy and Tim. On Saturday Topsy and Tim and Mummy set out for Bellford Fire Station.

There were lots of children at the fire
station. Firefighters in yellow helmets
were looking after them.

Topsy and Tim soon found Kerry
and her dad.
Kerry was waiting to go up on a
long turntable ladder. Topsy and
Tim wanted to go up too.
A firefighter helped them all into a
cage on the end of the ladder. He
gave them safety helmets to wear.

A firefighter at the back
of the appliance pulled
a lever and the ladder
started to go up.

It grew longer and longer and went higher and higher, until the people on the ground looked as small as toys.
"We hose water down on to burning buildings from up here," said the firefighter.
"And you rescue people from high windows and roofs," said Kerry.

When they came down from the
ladder, Mummy bought them each
a little firefighter's helmet.
"I'm going to be a firefighter when
I grow up," said Kerry.
"Can girls be firefighters?" asked
Topsy. "I don't think so," said Tim.

"Yes, they can!" said the lady who was selling the toy helmets.
"I'm a firefighter, just like Kerry's dad. Women can be firefighters, but they have to be as strong and as brave as the men."

To show how strong she was, she gave Tim a fireman's lift.

Kerry's dad took them to see how
the fire station worked.
"When there is a fire and
someone phones 999," he said,
"we get the message on a fax
machine. A loudspeaker tells
us where to go and which
appliances to take."

"Alarm bells ring and the firefighters run to the appliances. If they are upstairs they slide down a pole. It's quicker than running down the stairs."

Kerry's dad lifted the children into the cab of a big fire appliance. They pretended to drive to a fire.

Near the big fire appliance was a much smaller one. "Is that a baby fire engine?" asked Tim. "It's a van full of rescue equipment," said Kerry's dad. "We take it to accidents and rescue people from crashed cars and trucks."

Kerry's dad showed them the tall tower
where the firefighters practised with
their ladders and hoses.
"When we have finished we hang the
hoses in the tower to dry," he told them.
Next to the tower was a room that had
been on fire. It made their noses tickle.

"We make smoky fires in there," said Kerry's dad. "Then we practise putting them out and rescuing people. We have to wear masks and carry tanks of air on our backs, or we would choke."

Kerry took Topsy and Tim into a
showroom full of fire dangers. It
looked like an ordinary living room.
"See if you can spot where fires
could start," said Kerry.
Tim spotted a cigarette on an
armchair seat.
"That could start a fire," he said.

Topsy spotted a box of matches on the floor.
"A naughty little child might start a fire with those," she said.
"And that electric heater should be behind a fireguard," said Mummy.

Mummy spotted
more fire dangers
near a kitchen
stove. "Are smoke-
detectors any use?"
she asked Kerry's dad.
"I think I ought to get one."
Kerry's dad showed them a smoke-
detector and made it work. It made
loud BLEEP-BLEEP-BLEEP noises.

"If there was a fire in your home one night, the smoke-detector would wake you up," he said.
"We've got one," Kerry told Topsy.

It was time to go home, but before they went, Kerry's dad gave them one last treat.

It was a ride round the fire station yard on a children's fire appliance. The clever firefighters had made it specially for their open day.